SALTY D

Gloria Rand

ILLUSTRATED BY
Ted Rand

HENRY HOLT AND COMPANY
NEW YORK

"**H**i there, Zack! How's the boat builder?" asked the ferryboat ticket taker.

"Great! I've got the keel laid," answered Zack.

At the sound of Zack's voice, a puppy poked his nose out of Zack's parka pocket.

"Here's my new dog, Salty," smiled Zack. "I'm hoping he'll turn into a deep sea sailor, y'know, a real salty dog."

"A dog!" exclaimed the ticket taker. "Wouldn't a cat be a better sailor?"

"Could be, maybe," Zack answered, "but I'd rather have a salty dog crew for me any day."

"Well, O.K.," said the ticket taker, patting Salty's fuzzy head. "He should meet the Captain. Go on up to the wheelhouse."

The Captain was pleased to see Salty. "Needs to know my engineer. Take him below to the boiler room," commanded the Captain, handing Salty over to the first mate.

The engineer liked Salty very much. He introduced him to the oiler and all the deckhands.

"Salty has to go topside, cook's up there," one of the deckhands said, tucking Salty under his arm and heading for the galley on the passenger deck.

"What have we here?" asked the cook. "I've something just for you," she said, giving Salty a little treat.

Salty made a lot of friends in just one ferryboat ride.

When the ferry docked, Zack, with Salty back in his parka pocket, walked the short distance to the boatyard.

There Zack found a small cardboard box. He put shredded newspaper and soft wood shavings into the box. He also put in a blue dish filled with water and a red dish filled with puppy food.

"I'll be too busy building the boat to watch out for you," Zack explained as he lifted Salty into the box. "There are lots of dangerous places and things around a boat-yard that could mean trouble for a nosy puppy. You're much better off in here."

Salty didn't mind being in the box at all. He played with the shredded paper and
wood shavings. He ate his puppy food, he lapped up lots of water, and he took naps.

Weeks went by. The keel was laid and the boat framed, planked, and caulked. As the boat grew, Salty grew and the boxes grew.

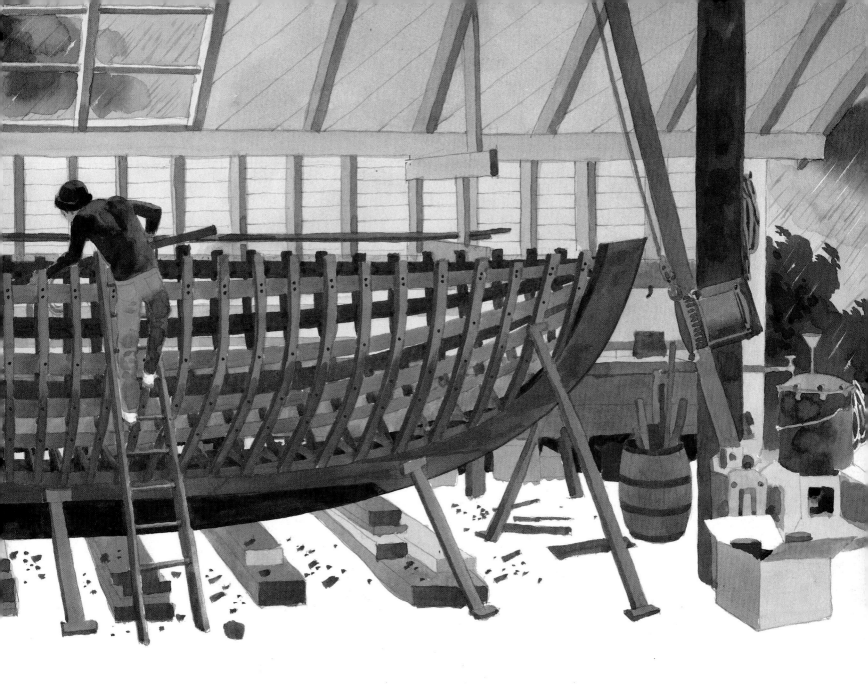

The weeks turned into months. Decking was put down and the cabin built. The boat had grown and Salty had grown. No cardboard box was big enough to hold Salty anymore.

So Salty was left at home alone all day. He had food and water, a snug doghouse in a large fenced yard. But he did not have Zack close by.

One day Salty decided to find Zack.
He dug out under the fence, and with
dirty paws and a dirty face ran to
the dock.

The ferryboat was about to leave.
Salty raced aboard.

When the boat docked, Salty dashed ashore and off to the boatyard as fast as he could go.

Zack couldn't believe his eyes. He picked Salty up and hugged him. "How did you get here?" Salty just licked Zack's face.

"I want you close by and quiet," Zack told Salty.

After a while Salty started to snoop around. Zack pointed toward the ferry dock. "Go home now, Salty."

Salty lay down. His ears drooped.

"I mean it, Salty! Go!" Zack said sternly.

Salty didn't want to leave, but he got up and slowly made his way back to the dock.

He waited patiently for the ferryboat, and when it arrived Salty went aboard and rode back home.

Salty visited Zack every day.

When it was sunny and warm, he rode up at the bow of the ferry's car deck, watching sea gulls and passing boats.

When it was raining and cold, he would sneak into the boiler room and sit by a warm engine, never bothering the busy engineer.

When he wanted a little something to eat, he sat outside the galley door.

When he felt important,
he rode in the wheelhouse with
the captain.

When he felt frisky, he tried to
help the deckhands keep the
ferryboat shipshape.

At the boatyard he made no
trouble. He learned to help
Zack, fetching tools and serving as
official guard dog.

Soon it was time to launch the sailboat.
It was an important and exciting day.
The boat was lowered into the water
and towed to the marina.

Next came stocking and outfitting the sailboat.

Salty waited outside the sail-makers' loft, where Zack picked up the finished sails.

He waited outside a store called "The Navigator," where Zack bought a compass, a sextant, and charts.

He waited outside the sporting goods store, where Zack purchased rods, reels, and line for ocean fishing.

He waited outside the supermarket, where Zack stocked up on canned, dried, and powdered foods.

But at the ship supply store where Zack got flags, lanterns, lines, fittings, and foul weather gear to wear on wet stormy days, Salty didn't wait outside.

"I've a surprise for you, Salty," Zack explained, holding open the store's front door.

Salty was fitted for a life vest. "In case you fall overboard, I want to be sure you stay afloat until I swing back to pick you up," Zack told him.

"We'll get you a safety harness, just like mine, for when there's a bad storm at sea. If you get washed overboard, you'll be tied to the boat and I'll haul in on the line and get you safely back on deck."

The boat was finished and ready for its shakedown cruise. Sails were rigged, fittings in place, all supplies aboard and stowed away.

The day of the shakedown was wet and windy. A perfect testing day.

Zack told Salty that they would sail out into the bay, check the compass, be certain the boat was watertight, try all the sails, and make sure the fittings and equipment were secure and working well.

They would also find out what kind of a sailor Salty would be.

All was shipshape, and Salty proved himself to be a very good sailor.

He loved the rough water, the cold wind, and the bouncy boat.

"You're smart, and you're going to be a great crew," Zack told Salty.

SALTY

A few days later, with sunny skies and a perfect light breeze, Zack and Salty set sail. Their friends crowded onto the dock, all cheering and waving. A flotilla of small boats, filled with more cheering and waving people, escorted them out into the bay, where the local fireboat was sending up arcs of spray in a watery salute.

Sitting just offshore was the ferryboat. Salty barked his excitement. Zack laughed.

As they sailed past the ferry, the ferry blew its whistle over and over again. The Captain and first mate waved from the pilothouse, the cook waved from the galley porthole, the engineer and oiler had come up from the boiler room and waved from the bow, the ticket taker waved from the bridge, and all the deckhands held up a big banner across the car deck that read: "HAVE A GOOD TRIP ZACK AND SALTY DOG!"

Salty stood at attention. He was on his way around the world.

Dedicated with great affection
to Elaine and Hans Jorgensen,
our true backup crew

Published by Henry Holt and Company, Inc.,
115 West 18th Street, New York, New York 10011.
Published in Canada by Fitzhenry & Whiteside Limited,
91 Granton Drive, Richmond Hill, Ontario L4B 2N5.

Library of Congress Cataloging-in-Publication Data
Rand, Gloria.
Salty dog / by Gloria Rand ; illustrations by Ted Rand.
Summary: Salty the dog helps his master build a sailboat.
[1. Dogs—Fiction.   2. Boats and boating—Fiction.
3. Sailboats—Fiction.]   I. Rand, Ted, ill.   II. Title.
PZ7.R1553Sal   1989
[E]—dc 19   88-13453

ISBN 0-8050-0837-3 (hardcover)
10 9 8 7 6 5 4 3 2 1
ISBN 0-8050-1847-6 (paperback)
10 9 8 7 6 5 4 3

Henry Holt books are available at special discounts
for bulk purchases for sales promotions, premiums,
fund-raising, or educational use. Special editions
or book excerpts can also be created to specification.

First published in hardcover in 1989 by
Henry Holt and Company, Inc.
First Owlet paperback edition, 1991

Printed in the United States of America